The Empty Couple

The Empty Couple

ONEAL WALTERS

The Empty Couple

Copyright @ 2021 Oneal Walters

All rights reserved.

eBook 978-0-9738573-3-7

Paperback Book 978-0-9738573-2-0

Hardcover Book 978-0-9738573-4-4

Redtail Turtle Publishing Inc.

Table of Contents

1

Turning the doorknob,
the closet door opens.
He sees only white and black hangers.
Wham! The closet door shuts. He yells,
"Where are my clothes?!"

Hearing the loud slam,
Ruth rushes upstairs from the kitchen
into the hallway, towards the master suite.
She stops within the doorframe
leaning backwards
and holding out a plate with a sandwich on it.
"They are in the washing machine," she explains.

He turns around, his facial expression ghostlike,
Ruth's heart beats rapidly against her chest
as she stares into his eyes, and then looks down.
He clenches his right fist, followed by the left one,
then stomps, charging towards her like an elephant.

Ruth steps back into the hallway, fear evident on her face.

"I w-w-ant you to have c-c-clean clothes for next w-w-weekkkk…,"

she stutters, raising one hand to cover the side of her face,

then she quickly adds,

"So the clothes can be ready when you need them."

"You can't do anything right!" he yells. "Only a stupid woman

would wash all my clothes at once." Grabbing the snack,

he strikes the plate with his fist.

The plate falls and shatters into pieces.

His reaction makes Ruth jump out of her skin.

She is thoroughly terrified.

"Look what you made me do! Clean it up.

All I wanted was clean clothes. You ruined my day."

He exits the hallway and goes downstairs,

leaving the house through the front door.

Tears stream down her cheeks.

Still shaking, Ruth leaves the hallway

and goes downstairs.

Walking into the kitchen,

she sees three empty bottles.

She slides her feet into slippers,

opens the closet door, and

grabs the broom and dustpan.

Returning to the broken plate and sandwich,

she sweeps up the mess.

2

Listening to music on the radio,
Ruth turns the volume up
because she is home alone.

Mouthing the words of the song,
she smiles and begins to dance.
Ruth is not a dancer,
but she enjoys her free time.
Apart from the radio playing, the house is silent.

The garage door opens.

Ruth turns off the music.
She runs into the kitchen and takes out a glass;
not just any glass, but his favorite one, with the maple leaf.
Ruth follows this obligatory routine whenever she hears him arriving.
He expects his glass to be filled with beer
every time he comes home after her in the evenings.

His keys unlock the door. Then he steps inside.

"Ruth, where are you?" Michael calls.
He drops his keys into his pocket,

using his foot as a door stopper.
He swings one six-pack into the house
and then picks up the second case.
"Come get my beer."

3

He smiles, holding his beer
like a lion with prey in his mouth.
He sits and turns on the TV.

Ruth brings in the case of beer,
throws the cardboard case in the recycle bin
and loads the new beer into the refrigerator.
She wipes the dripping glass cup,
picks it up, and follows his laughter.
He is watching comedy on TV.

"Do you want to start your own business?" she asks,
setting his glass next to him.

He opens another beer bottle and his smile turns cold.
"I'm meeting people in Blue," he answers. "Talking about jobs.
Nothing's happening. Doing all I can."

"You're lazy because you don't want to put in the effort,"
she replies.

"There is no such thing as a good woman anymore!" he says.
"Unemployment rate is increasing for full-timers.
The news is lying. I only see part-time jobs available.
No entrepreneurs are starting new businesses.
Daily, I see a lot of men facing unemployment.
Students are taking simple jobs from May to September
Companies are not hiring full-timers."
He gulps the beer and laughs at a joke on TV totally ignoring her.

Ruth sits on the single couch
her knees facing him.
She asks another question.
"Do you know how long it has been since you last worked?"

"I'm not counting," he replies. "I go to body shops every morning,
come back in the late evenings. I'm looking for new jobs.
The Collision Centre was my life; I loved it there.
We bought a new house and two new Lexus;
we both have savings.
Ruth, don't stress me out anymore."

She stares at him. "It's been five weeks.
I can't handle all the bills; I need you, Michael.
Can't you ask for your old job back?"

"I've been a mechanic for ten years," he replies, still watching TV.
"John Peters is a decent employer.
I was wrongly let go by his dumb son.
He's a jerk… nothing like his father.
Stop stressing me out.

4

Ruth sits back, unable to argue further.
Michael yawns loudly; his eyes are heavy with sleep.
After a while, she slowly walks upstairs.

A minute later, she returns with a folded blanket in her arms.
The TV is still on and Michael is asleep.
His beer bottles have fallen on the floor.

Ruth covers him with a blanket.
She looks down at him with regret.
She imagines him working again.

After ten minutes, she stops musing
and returns upstairs to bed.

On the living room floor are six empty beer bottles,
and on the wooden table, his empty glass.
Michael is asleep on the couch and only awakes
after the alarm-like sound begins,
the one that only occurs when there is no more
scheduled TV programming.

He stumbles over one bottle
and kicks another underneath the couch.
His balance awkward going up the stairs.

Entering the hallway,
he uses the wall for support.
Turning left to the master bedroom,
he stumbles in and yells "*Ahh! Ahhhhhhhhhhh!*"
like a wounded beast; a piece of shattered plate
has pierced his left foot, causing it to bleed.

"Ruth, you bitch!" he roars. "You ungrateful bitch."

6

Ruth awakens in bed.

She raises her head from the pillow,

lowers the covers, and sits up.

"Michael, what happened?" she asks.

"Please don't call me a bitch. And it's late,

I have to go to work in the morning."

She yawns, and feeling for the desk lamp, she turns it on.

She looks warily at his piercing eyes and his gorilla stance.

"I'm sorry, what happened?"

"You're trying to kill me!" he bellows. "You didn't clean up!"

He walks past the area where the plate fell.

His blood marks his path,

his weight firmly pressed on his right foot.

He travels towards Ruth's chest of drawers

and grabs the first and second items on top,

throwing them against the wall.

Smash!

"Please stop," Ruth begs. "I'm sorry. Please!
My mother gave me that vase as a present."

Smash!

Ruth jumps out of bed and faces him.
She is two steps away from being in direct contact.
"Why are you doing this to me?!" she yells.
"You're becoming a monster!"

Almost hidden in the dark,
he reaches over for her cell phone, exclaiming,
"I'm the victim! I'm the one bleeding.
If I'm a monster, you made me this way!"
He grips her cell and raises his hand high,
and then brings it straight down like a roller coaster.
Her cellphone falls and bounces off the floor in pieces.

"You're a monster!" she screams.
"Stop doing this to me!"
She charges at him, breaking through his cobra stare.
She pushes Michael with her right hand.
"I need my cell for work!"
When she tries to push him a second time,
he grabs her wrist.

"You're hurting me," she pleads. "Please stop.
Michael, you're really hurting me."

He grabs her other wrist,
and holds both, pulling them closer to his chest.
He snaps his lower back forward
and fully extends his arms.
Ruth falls backwards,
hitting her head on the bed.

7

"Mr. Christian wants you in his office now," Ashley says
as Ruth walks by her desk.
Ashley's desk is decorated with 15 souvenirs,
which landmark her lovely explorations,
a black phone, black keyboard, small white earphones
plus a black 24" gaming monitor.

"Do you know why?" Ruth asks.

"No clue. He's been calling you on your cell."

"My cell accidentally fell in the toilet."

"I hate it when that happens!" Ashley says.

"I read on the internet you can dry it out with rice."

Ruth fiddles with some documents in her hands.

"I will take those," Ashley says. "Go to Mr. Christian now."

"Thanks, Ashley."

8

Ruth slowly walks to Kevin's office.
She thinks about Kevin Christian
and what he could possibly want.

His door plate reads:
Kevin Christian
Senior Partner, Christian & Strong LLP.
Kevin sees her and smiles.
"Ruth, welcome," he says.
"I hope we are not keeping you too busy?"

"I'm not busy enough, sir," she assures him.

"No need to call me sir. This is an unofficial review.
We are watching your determination and results."

"We?" she asks.

"Yes, all of us," he says.
"Your non-billable hours are even higher than mine.
You work 12-hour days without taking a break.

Hope we haven't put too much strain on your relationship.
What is his name again? I remember he loves to drink."

"Michael…" she answers. "And he doesn't drink like he used to."

"Good, good." He smiles broadly. "Any plans for marriage yet?"

"No plans for marriage yet, sir… I mean, Kevin.
He and I won't be common law forever, though,
just have minor stuff to sort out and a new house."

Kevin Christian's smile fades.
Using his left and then right hand,
he intensely wipes away white flakes
that have settled on his dark blue suit.
"A beautiful woman like you should be off the market,"
Kevin advises.
"My wife and I often talk about how pretty you are.
Ruth, take it from me. Don't wait too long
to tell him how you really feel and what you need.
Love, like life, must be a continuous progression.
Let him know a 4-year wait is too long."

Kevin Christian clears his throat.
"In your first year,
you became a Non-Equity Partner," he says.
"In your second year,
your performance was excellent
and you're currently a home owner, eh? Good, good.
Is there anything that I can do for you, Ruth?
I offered an assistant on two occasions."

"It's not necessary," she answers. "I love what I do, sir."

"I insist," he says. "That's that. From next week, you will have one. You will go home like everyone else."
He leans back into his chair and shares a deeper smile.

"Okay, thanks," she says with a grimace.

"Smile, you make it seem like I'm pulling teeth in here." He laughs.

"Funny, sir. I'm happy for all your help."

9

"Welcome back! What did Mr. Christian need?" Ashley inquires.

"It was some good and some bad news," Ruth answers.

Ruth leaves and heads into her office.

Just before she closes the door,
Ashley informs her,
"Michael called and left you a message.
He said he will be home late."

"Okay," Ruth replies. "Thanks for letting me know."

"Great," Ashley says. "Is he working again?"

"Not that I know of," Ruth replies. "He didn't say so, at least."

Ruth closes the door and cries.

A while later, Ashley knocks on the door.
"Hon," she says, "here is a new cell phone.
Your number remains the same.

Stay away from open toilets."

She places the cell on Ruth's desk.

"Thanks, Ashley," Ruth answers with a wan smile.

10

Pulling up to the curb,
Ruth parks and leaves the car on.
She opens the mailbox;
several letters await her.

She opens Michael's mail in the car:
Final notice - pay now - $900.11
to prevent phone service disconnection.
Tears fall and soften the mail as she carries it into the house.

She reads the second letter:
Pay immediately, $1262.19 car payment.

She reads the third letter, which is hers:
Property tax $708.00 due.

She stomps her feet on the ground, facing the sky.

She screams out loud,

"Dear Lord, our mortgage is due soon.

Help us, please. We need You, amen!"

5:40pm, Ruth goes home to change her clothing.

11

A male customer opens the door for Ruth.
She steps onto the black and white mat
that reads: John Peters Auto Collision Centre.

"Thank you very much," she says with a nod.

He nods his head in return, smiles and then sits
beside a woman who only stares at Ruth.
The woman places her left hand on top
of his right hand, her wedding ring sparkling.

Ruth sees a crowded waiting room.
She hears, "Always low prices!" from the TV.

There is a little boy playing with crayons.
"I'm hungry," he whines. "Can we go?"

"We'll be leaving very soon," his father reassures.
The man's attention shifts to Ruth as she waits.

Ruth hears a conversation directly ahead.

"It will cost you $750.00," the mechanic says.

"But with aftermarket parts I can save you $150.00.
Let's make the call now."

"That's a lot of money," the customer says.

"Can I get a written quote?"

"Yes," the mechanic agrees.

"But if you get it done cheaper, it will cost you more later."

"I'll do it," the customer replies, placing his keys on the counter.

"Make your call.
She's the black one." He points. "Parked over there."

The mechanic takes the keys off the counter,
hangs them on his wall of keys and says,
"Okay, thanks, sir. Please have a seat."

The customer sits next to a tank full of goldfish.

Ruth walks off the mat, *tap, tap, tap, tap.*
The mechanic sees her heels, long smooth legs,
a dark blue skirt, white slim fit V-neck blouse,
and a blue bra that peeks slightly from beneath.

"Can I help you?" he asks.

"Yes, please," Ruth says. "May I speak to Jason?"

"He's busy," the mechanic says, shaking his head.
"But I'm available to help you."

"I need to speak with Jason," Ruth says. "I can wait."

"He's very busy, love," the mechanic replies.
"But I can address your every need."

"I'm not interested. Go get Jason!"

12

In the moment before her tears start falling,
Ruth makes eye contact with another mechanic.
He immediately stops vehicle repair,
comes over to her, and interrupts the first mechanic.

"Don't you know who she is?" the second mechanic says.
"She's Michael's girlfriend!"

"Oh my God…" the first mechanic says.
"Tell Michael we all say hi."

"Ruth, what brings you here?" the second mechanic asks.

"I need to speak to Jason," Ruth says. "It's urgent."

The mechanic leaves and enters an office.
There is mumbling, nothing that Ruth can decode;
she is too far away to hear their words.

A confident-looking man walks towards Ruth.

"How can I help you, Ruth?" Jason asks.

"It's been a long time since we last met."

"It's about Michael," she says. "No one is hiring him.

Could you please give him his job back?

Financially, we are having a difficult time.

Jason, he will work long hours or take any job."

She moves closer to Jason and whispers in his ear.

"He would kill me if he knew I was here with you.

Please don't tell him! Will you please help us?"

"Ruth," he says, keeping eye contact,

"Michael has known my father for over 10 years.

He was regarded as a close family friend.

Then he disrespected my father and me

by arriving to work drunk.

I had no choice but to terminate him."

Ruth falls to her knees.

Jason looks stern as he informs her,

"I gave him three warnings, Ruth,

but the decision was made by my father.

Michael bankrupted his reputation."

13

Jason extends his hands to Ruth, saying,
"A pretty flower should not bend to the ground."

Ruth holds his hands and relies on him for support.

Jason notices her bruised wrists as she stands.
"What happened to your wrists?" he asks.
"Did Michael do this to you?"

"I made a mistake coming here," Ruth says.
"Michael is a good man.
He used to drink.
He wouldn't hurt me.
You turned your back on a kneeling woman.
I hope you never marry so she will never feel my pain.
Michael gave his entire life to your family for 10 years.
It was all for nothing. Jason, you spat in his face.
You bankrupted us because you lack forgiveness."
She storms out of the workshop.

14

In the car, Ruth cries and prays:

"Oh, Lord, this weight is too much to bear.

The heaviness of my pain is crushing my chest.

Success at work feels like nothing is gained

when my family is crippled with pain.

Forgive me and conquer my enemy.

Beer is my enemy, so separate us, Lord.

Please don't allow defeat to destroy me, Lord.

I've fought enough, can't fight anymore. Amen."

15

"Michael will not be a victim anymore," Ruth chants.
She removes six beers from the refrigerator,
and pours all of them down the kitchen sink.

"Michael will not be a victim anymore,"
she continues chanting as she goes into the living room.
She takes up his favorite glass,
returns to the kitchen and hides it behind antique plates.

She collects the six empty bottles from the floor.
Afterwards she turns on the radio
and hears Nomi the Goddess singing,
"Love you babe, never let me go."

Ruth grabs all of Michael's clothes from the dryer.
She places them back onto the black and white hangers.
From upstairs, she can still hear the words of the song.

Ruth goes into the kitchen and uncorks a bottle of wine.
She pours a full glass and enjoys the first sip.
Then she dances slowly, finding her rhythm.

16

Minutes later, Ruth lies in bed.
She takes another sip of wine.
After the fifth sip, she replaces the sim card
from her new cell with her old cell's sim.

After the tenth sip,
she throws away the remaining cell pieces
broken due to Michael's rage
and mops the bedroom floor.

The radio plays a song by Sandra Richards.
The tempo of the song calms her;
her breathing is peaceful.

After the fifteenth sip,
she scribbles on a notepad:
When you read this please wake me up.
we need to talk if you're up for it.
Love, Ruth

She changes into an emerald green outfit,
falling asleep afterwards with her open palms
touching her lips as if she is a saint praying.

17

"You can't do everything alone," Michael cautions.
"Only a stupid woman
carries a heavy load without asking for help.
I don't want you to strain yourself."

The plate shatters into pieces on the floor.
"Look at what I've done!" he says. "I'll clean it up."

"Ruth," he calls. "Where are you?"
"I'm in the living room, hon," she replies.

"Come into the kitchen, please," he says.

Ruth enters the kitchen and is surprised
by an antique vase with a dozen red roses.

"Do you want to start your own business?" she asks.

He opens a beer bottle, sips, then frowns.
"I don't like the taste." Setting aside the bottle, he says,
"I have been meeting with investors,
registering a business name,
talking with several banks.
I wanted all of this to be a surprise.
Leaving John Peters Collision Centre
was the best thing that happened to me."

18

"*Wait, when did you get engaged?*" *Kevin Christian says.* "*Congrats!*"

"*This morning!*" *Ruth says.* "*It's like a dream come true.*
We don't have a wedding date yet, but we both hate
living together as common-law partners, so he popped
the question and I said yes!
Michael has started a new body shop,
and we recently bought a house."

"*Ruth,*" *Kevin says,* "*in your first year,*
you became a Non-Equity Partner.
In your second year,
we have decided for you to become an Equity Partner."
He gives Ruth a firm handshake.
"*Your performance has been excellent*
and your fiancé has started a business;
we will support you both by referring our clients to him.
Also, I insist that all partners have an assistant."

"*Sure,*" *Ruth replies.* "*I suggest Ashley. Let's send her to school.*"

19

The young man parks Michael's car and hands him the keys.
"You'll be okay, sir?" he asks.

"Sure... go on... home," Michael mumbles.

The young man slams the door to Michael's Lexus,
runs to a car waiting behind
and jumps in.

"Who was that?" his friend asks.

"Michael," the young man says.

"He always used to fix my dad's car."
"Why was he alone at the bar?" his friend asks.

"I've heard he is always there," replies the young man.
"Every day, since,
well, since he was fired for drinking."

"Fired!" his friend responds. "Michael's a loser.
He should get a job like the rest of us."

The young man points at the house and car.
"Look at his house and his vehicle.
He has more than both of us combined."

His friend frowns.
"No employment and spending every day at the bar?
Soon he'll be emailing us a resume for a job."

20

Music is coming from inside the house.

He fumbles his keys and they drop onto the cement.

He slides his greasy hands along the ground

until he finds them, then puts the keys into the door.

Inside, he hears, "*Loving you has torn me apart.*"

He stumbles past the couch to the radio.

Yanking on the cord, he unplugs it,

then removes his shoes and lies on the couch.

21

One thing is clear, he thinks.
Because of Ruth's radio,
I have a terrible headache.

He drags himself upstairs,
then goes inside the bedroom.
He sees a wine glass, an open Bible,
and a piece of paper on the Bible.

Ruth is wearing an emerald green outfit
that dimly reminds him of his birthday.
The constant throbbing in his head
disconnects him from the memory of that night.
He reads and crushes Ruth's note,
tossing it towards the dresser
with the intensity of a Major League pitcher.
He picks up the Bible and throws it upward.
Gravity grabs it and sends it crashing;
the spine splits on contact with the hardwood floor.

22

"Hon, I had a wonderful dream, or maybe two of them," Ruth says,
stretching in bed and smiling at her memories.
"They were signs that things will be better."
Ruth turns around and doesn't see Michael;
his side of the bed looks untouched.

Where is he? she thinks.
She returns to her lamp and table, no note.
He must have read my note. Why didn't he wake me?
Doesn't he find me beautiful? I'm beautiful... aren't I?
Where's my Bible? She looks on his table, nothing.

She looks on the floor beside the lamp, nothing.
She surveys the dresser, nothing. She slides off the bed
and walks towards the double doors; she sees the split Bible.
She gasps for air and feels tightness in her upper back.
She feels intense pressure mounting her chest.
"Michael! Michael! Please help me!" she yells.

She falls to the floor.

23

Ruth's body lies lifeless.
Her spirit unglues itself from her body.
It floats towards the Bible and tries to pick it up.

A spirit enters the room.
Ruth stares at her unmoving body.

Am I dead? she thinks.

"Yes, you are dead, Ruth," replies the spirit.

How can you hear me?

"All of us share a vibration of positive energy," explains the spirit.
"When you think, we can all hear you."

Then why are you talking?

"Because you are not able to hear us yet," the spirit responds.
"You have died but it is not yet your time, Ruth.
You still have a few attachments."

Does Michael think I'm beautiful? Ruth wonders.

"Such desires and answers hold no value here.
If beauty existed here, it would be a personal choice.
Beauty by the standards of others is bondage," the spirit explains.

24

Michael passes the last step.
He walks through the hallway,
large pictures on both sides:
six framed pictures of him in uniform,
each taken at John Peters Collision Centre.

"Ruth, I had a busy night. What is it?" he asks.
"I have to leave soon. I bet you are wasting my time."

He turns into the room. "Where's my favorite glass?"

He sees Ruth's body lying on the floor, chest forward.

"Ruth, get up," he says.

He stands in the doorframe.
Then he runs and holds her—she's warm.

"Ruth! Ruth!" he yells.

He looks at the split Bible near her.

"Oh, no, this can't be!" he cries.
"Take me. I'm the worthless piece of… Have mercy on her.
Ruth, wake up."

He kisses her cheek.

"Please wake up!"

He lifts her effortlessly into his arms. Then he carries her to the bed,
takes out his cell, and dials 911.

25

"Not much time remains," the spirit warns.
"You must depart from here.
You must go directly inside your body
before you suffer physical damage."

The spirit floats over Ruth's body.
Ruth follows the spirit.

Michael hears the ambulance.
He leaves Ruth and runs downstairs.

How do I get back into my body? she thinks.

The spirit says, "Just go into your body; you need to be there."

Why should I need to be with a man who hurts me? Ruth thinks.
Why should I live each day being unloved?
Why doesn't he hate being unemployed and find a job?
No, this place is better than where I came from.

Two more spirits float into the room and watch.

"Your silence causes much time to be lost," says the spirit.

The three spirits point at her body together.

You didn't hear my thoughts before? Ruth thinks.

"We communicate only on positive vibrations," explains the spirit.
"If your thoughts are outside of this wave,
I am not be able to hear or respond to you.
You need to leave now. Get into your body
and be restored to what you call normal."

What will happen to me? Ruth wonders.

"They may call it a miracle."

The emergency crew enters the room.

Ruth floats directly into her body.

26

Ruth awakens
and sees Michael and the all-male ambulance crew.

"How do you feel?" the lead paramedic asks.

"I feel great," she answers, and smiles.

"Could you tell me what happened?"

"I suppose I was tired and fainted," she answers.

"Can I ask what your name is?" he inquires.

"Ruth."

"Where are you right now?"

Ruth looks around.
"Inside my bedroom."

"Do you feel any pain?" he asks.

"I feel good," she replies.

The first paramedic performs tests on Ruth,
while the other crew member provides the equipment he needs.

"Can you stretch your arms?"

"Yes," she answers raising her arms above her head;
the two men immediately spot her bruised wrists.

"How do your arms feel?" the lead paramedic asks.

"I told you, I feel good," Ruth answers.

"Can you tell me what happened here?" he asks,
pointing to her wrist.

27

Two officers enter the bedroom;
the second crew member speaks to them.

"Is it okay if I talk to her alone?" the officer asks.

"Yes, it is," the man answers.

"Why alone?" Michael asks. "I called the ambulance."

"Do as he says," the second officer instructs. "Calm down, sir."
The four men leave the bedroom and wait in the hallway.

Ruth and the first officer are inside the bedroom.

In the hallway, the second officer asks, "Wild party last night?"

"No, officer," Michael answers.

"There were six bottles in the kitchen. Are they all yours?"

"Officer, I didn't drink any of those," Michael replies.

"Do you expect me to believe Ruth drank them all?"
The second officer asks.

"Officer, I don't know how they got there," Michael responds.

"Here's what I think," the second officer says. "You drank a lot;
six empty bottles show that. Ruth drank wine;
her wine glass in the bedroom shows that.
Yesterday, you had a romantic night planned;
her emerald outfit that she's wearing shows that.
You were angry at her; the torn Bible shows that.
So, it was an accident. You had too much to drink.
Tell me your side before we discover it.
What went wrong this morning?"

"Officer, I never touched her," Michael answers.
"I may have saved her life.
Why would I want to harm her?"

"Sir, I will be honest with you," the second officer says.
"I've seen you drinking alone in the bars.
You always refuse to buy girls drinks.
You appear to be a caring guy,
greasy marks on your hands,
perhaps hard working.
So I won't ask if you hurt her.
Did you accidentally push Ruth?"

"Officer, I'm not the type," Michael exclaims.
"I don't even watch cop shows.

I'm non-violent."

"Tell me, how did the Bible get on the floor?"
the second officer questions.

"Officer, I don't remember. I called 911," Michael says.

"Why do you think Ruth cried earlier?"

"Because she is happy to be alive," Michael replies.

"If the crumbled paper on the floor
reveals a different story about yesterday,
we will be going to the police station," the second officer warns.

28

In the bedroom,
the officer stands by the foot of the bed as he speaks with Ruth.
"You are safe now," the officer says. "So tell me what happened."

"I am safe, thanks to Michael," Ruth answers.

"Then why were you crying?"

"I was just overwhelmed with work and finances," she answers.

"Has he ever hurt you? Even if it was accidental?" the officer asks.

"He gets frustrated because he's not working."

"Tell me what happened this morning," the officer says.

"I guess I fainted due to the stress of everything,"
she says feebly.

"Has his frustration ever been expressed physically?"
the officer asks.

"He is a misunderstood man who doesn't deserve jail," Ruth replies.
"I suggest," the officer says, "that you spend today and overnight
with a friend."

"I don't have any friends. I don't have anywhere to go."
Frustration is evident in her voice.

"A co-worker is acceptable. Just go someplace else,"
the officer advises.

"I could spend a night with my coworker Ashley," Ruth muses.

"Good. Pack some things and go to Ashley."

"She's at work. Oh, I'll be late for work... I'm a mess," Ruth says.

"You're fine," he says kindly. "Pack a few things. We will wait."

Ruth gets up and begins to pack a small bag.

She texts Ashley:
Emergency - can I spend the day with you?

Ashley replies:
Come in today and then we'll take the day off.

The officer watches Ruth reading the text message.
"Have your plans been confirmed?" the officer asks.

"Yes, I'll be spending the night with her," Ruth answers.

The officer opens the door.

"If she is cleared by you—"
The ambulance crew nods so the officer continues,
"Ruth will be leaving and will return in a few days."

"Ruth, what did you tell them?!" Michael yells.

The officer steps between Michael and Ruth.
He stands in the doorframe.

Facing Ruth, he suggests,
"Make an appointment with your doctor."
The ambulance crew leaves.

"Michael," the officer says, "follow me downstairs.
Sorry that you are not employed.
As a man, I know how difficult it is."
The officer's left hand passes over his face,
smothering fresh tears.

"My non-speaking father had a mental illness.
The bloody savage ended the life of my mother
when I was 7.
I heard each step from his heavy boots
as he descended down the wooden stairs.
I followed his red footprints backwards into the bedroom.
Blood everywhere. My mother never woke up."

The officer awkwardly pauses.

"You have a nice house
and a woman who cares about you.
It would be unfortunate
if your actions yesterday
caused you to lose everything.
I'm warning you," the officer continues.
"If I have to come back for any reason,
you will be coming with us."

29

Ruth lays her already-full cream hobo-style handbag on the bed.
She searches under the bed and finds a white duffle bag
and packs it with clothes to last a week.
She lays this bag beside the smaller handbag on the bed.

Ruth enters the washroom.
She rushes to apply her makeup.
She smiles, looking at herself,
"I'm so embarrassed.
I wish I had changed last night."

The officer waits in the bedroom.
"We see many strange things every week.
Your clothing is not one of them," the officer says.

Ruth returns to the bedroom,
picks up her white bag
and re-enters the washroom.
She changes into tight blue jeans
and a white and pink V-neck top.
Visible underneath her top is a black bra.

Ruth heads back into the bedroom.

What shoes should I wear? she thinks.

She picks up her white sandals

tries them on, and walks around the bedroom a bit.

Then she takes them off and tries on the black sandals.

She returns to the white sandals and smiles.

Looking at Ruth, fully dressed, the officer says,

"You look like a different woman."

Ruth smiles shyly as they walk out of the room.

30

Ruth's cell rings. She sees that she has received several texts.
It's Ashley messaging.

It reads: *Mr. Christian asked if you're coming in today.*
I told him you are taking a personal day
and that I will be taking one with you.
Hope this is okay. Come soon, okay?

Ruth drops her cell into her handbag.
She stares at the torn Bible on the floor.
The officer picks it up and gives it to her.
Ruth puts it into her duffle bag.

"Is that Michael?" the first officer asks.
"If he threatens you, in any way,
at any time, let me know."

Ruth smiles at his protective nature.
He stands perfectly still, sweat visible on his forehead,

his back against the double doors,
and his chest towards her.

"It's Ashley. I'm late for work," she replies.

"You should leave the premises now," he advises.

31

Ruth sits inside her car.
The white Lexus is parked inside the garage.
The officer stands outside the vehicle and watches.

Ruth holds and opens one letter.
It reads: *Property tax - $708.00 due.*
A wound re-opened, her tears fall.
Crying, she lowers the tinted window,
takes the remaining letters and asks,
"Could you give these to him?"

The officer takes Michael's letters.
"Okay," he replies.

Ruth pulls down the sun visor to look in the mirror;
she pulls out a tissue and pats her face.
Seeing the not-so-perfect condition of her face in the mirror,
she cries, "I just put on my makeup."

"Michael may try to contact you," the officer says.
"You have to minimize your contact with him.
Stay away until you are ready to return."

Ruth smiles and gives an affirmative nod.

Then she winds up the driver's-side window,

waves goodbye to the officer, and slowly drives away.

32

Ruth texts Ashley:
I'm parked outside.

Ashley arrives at the main doors.
She uses her hands to block the sun
as she walks over to Ruth's car.

Ruth lowers the tinted window slightly.
Showing only part of her face to Ashley, she asks,
"It's been a long morning; can we go somewhere?
I'll call you. Where did you park?"

Ashley smiles as she points at a dusty black Honda Accord.
"Over there," she says. "I should have taken it to the car wash."
She laughs as she begins to walk away.

Ruth calls Ashley as a thought strikes her.

"Hello," Ashley says, picking up right away.

"Don't you think I should see Mr. Christian before we leave?"
Ruth says.

"You don't have to worry. Mr. Christian approved your time off
and my sick time for a few days," Ashley informs her.

Ruth waits for Ashley to get to her car.
"Why did you say a few days off?" Ruth asks.

Ashley looks back when she notices
Ruth's vehicle isn't moving.
"You work 12 hours days," Ashley replies.
"You're rarely late for work; today was unreal.
Maybe you need a few days off for girl bonding.
Where do you want to go?"
Ashley gets into her car and starts the engine.

"Your place," Ruth answers.

"My place?" Ashley says. "Okay, cool. Sure.
I wasn't expecting a guest today.
Hope my place isn't too messy for you.
Will Michael be coming over tonight?"

"I'm sorry for pulling you into this," Ruth says.
"Michael is the reason we are here.
You're so sweet for taking a day off with me."
Ruth drives closer to Ashley's vehicle.
She flicks her lights; Ashley takes the lead.

"Stress is dense; this one, I can't fight through," explains Ruth

"I listen to music to dance my way through it.

Do you have a radio at your place?"

33

Ashley turns off the street into a gated complex.
"You live here?" Ruth asks.

"Yep. I have to warn you," Ashley says.
"The guard is very procedure oriented.
Just clearly state: a guest,
my name, your name and #1003.
Then I'll show you to visitor parking."

"Is everything okay, Ms. Ashley?" the guard asks.
"You have returned sooner than usual."

"Everything is great," Ashley says. "Just taking time off.
I have one guest; her name is Ruth."

"When are you expecting her?" he asks.

"She is behind me, silly," Ashley says, laughing.

"All right, Ms. Ashley. Enjoy your day," the guard replies.

"Same to you!" Ashley responds.

The gate opens and Ashley drives through.
The gate closes and Ruth approaches.
She lowers the window to see a short man
wearing a security guard uniform
and a walkie talkie on his left side.

"What is the purpose of your visit?
Who are you here to see?
What is your name?
Where is she located?" he asks.

Ruth says, "A guest, Ashley, Ruth, #1003."
"Ms. Ashley prepared you for this visit," he responds.
The gate opens and Ruth drives into the complex.

"You did great! They are super security conscious here,"
Ashley informs Ruth.
"Follow me. I'll show you where to park."

34

"Who lives here?" Ruth asks.

"Most of the residents are in their thirties
but a lot of new people are in their twenties," Ashley answers.

Ashley and Ruth wait in the elevator.

"Aren't you 20? How can you afford this?" Ruth asks.

"Excuse me?" Ashley answers.

Ruth raises her hands to her heart.
"I didn't mean to offend you; I'm sorry," Ruth says.
"I just know how challenging expenses can be."

"I'm only kidding, okay?" Ashley responds.
"I've invited many friends over,
but you are the only one to ask that.
I'm 22. I own this condo apartment;
perhaps I'm the youngest in the building.

It's cool and fun to live here.
I love it.
I bought it when I was 20.
Out of a negative situation, create a positive.
This is how I view life."

The elevator door opens;
Ashley leads Ruth to door #1003.
They go inside the apartment.

35

"My father had no siblings,
and he got married and had two children:
the oldest, a boy, and me, the girl," Ashley says.
"He taught my brother, 'Protect your sister'
and taught me, 'Love your brother.'
He used games, creative stories, or
made us write stories about family unity.
My father saw an unfulfilled need,
and he opened a business to solve this need.
Then he opened a second business.
The first business is located in Lock
and the other is in Blue.
He solved the challenges in his businesses
and his family was rewarded for his persistence.
By my tenth birthday, he was very successful.
Soon after my 20th birthday, his life was taken by cancer.
My mom always says to remember the toys, clothes,
flight destinations and paid tuitions.
She says our father loved us dearly."

"I'm sorry," Ruth interrupts.

"No, wait," Ashley replies. "It's okay.
At the age of ten, I lost my father.
He became a hostage to what he created.
He obsessed over his success and creating more success;
his two children were replaced by his two businesses.
When I was 20, cancer claimed him,
and on that day my brother cried.
He admires and copies my father's determination.
I lost an absent father who constantly gave me money.
I didn't cry.
I won't cry that it's not fair.
Luckily, also at the age of 20,
my father willed us his businesses.
My brother was excited; he's a mirror image of my father.
He manages both businesses today.
I enjoy the simple things.
I help him casually through email.
My brother ensures I receive a salary.
I receive more money than I need monthly,
so I'm at the law firm because I enjoy it."

Adding the last bit of information, Ashley giggles.

36

Ruth sits on the tan leather couch.

"Can I offer you something to drink?" Ashley asks.

"No, thanks," Ruth answers.

Ashley sits beside her.

"I'm not being honest with you," Ruth says.
"You have been very open with me.
Thank you for inviting me into your home."

Ruth leans slightly away from Ashley.

"My cell didn't fall in the toilet," Ruth says quietly.
"Michael broke it."

"How did it happen?" Ashley asks.

"He threw it against the floor," replies Ruth.

"He also broke my vase. It was a gift from my mother.

He's a drunken, angry, needy monster."

"Is this the reason why you always work late?" Ashley asks.

Ruth begins to cry.

"I am praised so much at work," says Ruth.

"I am despised so much at home.

I feel the hurt more than the love.

I'm stuck with a man who doesn't love me."

37

Ashley moves closer to Ruth, and hugs her tight.

"That's why I don't have a boyfriend," Ashley says.
"I'm happy not being stressed by boys.
Happier discovering more of the world.
I enjoy building life experiences."

Ashley releases Ruth from the hug and sits.

"You are pretty," Ashley says.
"You can have any guy you want."

"Thanks." Ruth forces a smile
as she looks around the living room.
"You have so many books," she says.

"Yes, all of them are by women authors," Ashley answers.
"I also have several self-defense books."

She gets to her feet. "Stand up," she tells Ruth.
"Now try to punch me."

Ruth tries to punch Ashley,
but Ashley blocks the punch.
Ruth tries a few more times,
but each time Ashley blocks.

"How are you doing that?" Ruth asks.

"I'll show you," Ashley answers.

Ashley turns her back to Ruth.
"Now grab me from behind," Ashley instructs.

"What do you want me to do?" Ruth says.

"Grab me, headlock me, choke me!" Ashley instructs.

Ruth grabs her in a headlock.

"When this happens, just do this and this," Ashley advises,
pushing her elbow back and then extending her arm down
until her fist meets Ruth's lower belly.

"No one will let go if you do that, Ashley," Ruth says, laughing.

"I did it softly," Ashley replies. "When you need to do it,
put all your body into the punches.
Let's try it again!"

38

A movie is playing on Ashley's large laptop.

"Ashley, don't you feel alone?" Ruth asks.

"My friends come over all the time," Ashley answers.

Ruth stands up. She walks around the living room,
while Ashley remains seated.

"Why don't you want a boyfriend?" Ruth asks.

"I just don't need a relationship to make me happy
right now," Ashley replies.
"It's 'discovering what makes me happy' time.
And when I've completed my 'me discoveries',
then I will begin my 'us discoveries' with a boyfriend.
What is going to happen with you and Michael?"

"Maybe being away from him for a while will change him,"
Ruth says.
It's frustrating because I might lose the house."

"Not while I'm here," Ashley says. "It's girl bonding, remember?"

"What does girl bonding mean?" Ruth asks.

Ashley gets up and leaves without any response.
She goes into a dark room, and turns the light on.

A few minutes pass,
Ruth ignores Ashley's absence
as she watches the thriller showing on the laptop.

Ashley returns with a check.
She folds it and gives it to Ruth.

"I can't accept this," Ruth says, trying to hand it back.

"Open it, okay?" Ashley says. "Please."

Ruth opens the check.
It's addressed to her.
The amount reads: $10,000.00.

She is flabbergasted.

39

Kevin, Ashley, and Ruth arrive to work at the same time.

Kevin walks to the main door
in a black suit with a white dress shirt.
His watch reflects sunlight into Ruth's eyes.
Ruth looks away.
Ashley is closer to Kevin;
Ruth follows behind her.

Kevin grins.
"Ruth, it's good to see you're back.
It seems nothing will keep you away.
If you're not too busy this morning,
come to my office at 9:10am please."

"I will be there sir," Ruth answers.

"Good, good," Kevin replies.

The morning flies by and Ruth soon finds herself at Kevin's doorway.

"Ruth, welcome," he says. "Come in and sit.
Our firm has a well-respected reputation,
and you are an excellent addition to this company.
We value and appreciate your determination,
and we reward those who make our business do well.
Now you're really going to be busy," he jokes.

"In front of you are legal documents.
We are offering you an Equity Partnership.
Ruth, you are consistently ahead of the rest.
We would be pleased if you accepted this offer."

Smiling from ear to ear, Ruth stands up and answers, "I accept!"
She holds out her hand to Kevin.
"Thank you very much, sir."

"Wait, now," Kevin says.
"There are three conditions you should be aware of:
One, your assistant will start tomorrow.
Two, only work 12-hour days if you need to.
Three, you must accept your salary bump.
It's none of my business;
however, I am good friends
with one of the officers
who came over to your house.
Maybe this will help things.
Do you accept the conditions?"

"Yes sir," Ruth answers.

Kevin extends his hand to Ruth.

"Your promotion is effective immediately. once you sign."

40

"Thanks for being a friend, Ashley," Ruth says,
turning into her driveway
and putting the car in park.

"No worries," Ashley says over the phone
as she pulls up behind Ruth.
"Girl bonding, okay?
You have a nice house."

"This old thing," Ruth says,
laughing as they head towards the house.

Ruth opens the front door.
She sees:
beer bottles broken on the floor,
her radio smashed into pieces,
her two side tables crushed.
However her TV is untouched.
Also, a red line has been sprayed on the walls
from the kitchen all the way upstairs.

"You've been robbed!" Ashley exclaims.

"No, this is Michael," Ruth answers.

A look of shock and confusion was evident on Ashley's face.

Ruth walks inside the house.
She looks at the kitchen:
all the plates are broken,
all the regular glasses are also broken.
His beer glass is on the counter;
milk is also on the counter.
Forks and spoons are scattered across the counter.
There is thawed frozen food on the floor.

"He's crazy," Ashley says. "Maybe we should call the police."

"No," Ruth says. "If you want to go, you can."

"I'm not leaving you alone here," Ashley says.
"Let's clean up.
Ruth, where are the knives?"

41

Ruth and Ashley clean everything,
placing the mess into large black garbage bags
and taking them outside.

Ruth goes upstairs, Ashley following behind her.
Everything seems normal.
Then she goes into the bedroom;
it doesn't look normal.

What is that in the bed? she thinks.
Her side of the bed has an unexpected lumpiness.
Ruth carefully removes the top sheet
and sees every knife stabbed into the mattress.

"I'm going to call the police now," Ashley says.
"I'm taking pictures of this."

"No," Ruth says. "Don't call the police."

Ashley uses her cellphone to takes pictures
and helps Ruth remove the knives.

"Let's go back to my place," says Ashley.
"What if he comes home?"

When they've finished straightening up,
Ruth leads her friend to the door.
"Thanks, Ashley," she says. "I will see you tomorrow."
"Are you nuts?" Ashley says. "Michael is a psycho.
I won't leave you alone."
"Please go," Ruth says. "If you stay here, it will be worse."

Reluctantly, Ashley leaves the house and drives away.

Ruth turns off the lights and waits.

42

Ruth hears Michael's slow heavy footsteps.

He arrives in the hallway, calling out, "Where are you, Ruth?"
He pushes open the door and sees no one, only darkness.
"Where are you hiding? I know you're here."
His fingers turn the switch on. They stare at each other.

"Welcome back home," Michael jeers.

He staggers into the bedroom.

"It destroyed all that I have," Ruth says scornfully.
"I accept the truth; it doesn't love me.
It's an evil, selfish, monster!"

He fumbles in his pocket,
pulls out a steel pocket knife, and opens it.
"Do you like my new tool?" Michael taunts.

Ruth stands firm, clearly unbothered.

He drops the open knife onto the floor.
"You left me alone. You left me,
so I made a welcome home surprise."
He moves further inside the bedroom.
"All of this is your fault.
You are responsible for my pain."

He swings once at her and misses.
He steps closer and swings again.
Ruth blocks his punch.
He swings again;
she deflects his punch.
He slowly backs away.

Ruth smiles and relaxes.

43

He flips down the light switch. Darkness.
She moves slowly with her hands out,
breathing heavily in the dark.
She smells his alcoholic breath;
he's very close to her.

Wham!! Ruth drops to the floor.
"Bull's eye, dodge that one," he taunts.
He feels around the floor, finds her leg,
grabs it to pull her close, punches her stomach,
then punches her twice in the face with his sandpaper-rough fist.

"Don't hurt me anymore," she pleads.
She pats the floor searching for the pocket knife.

Michael pulls her up.
Holding her arms behind her back,
he presses her face against the cold window.
"You took your Bible, but I got your radio." Michael laughs.
"Now, say goodnight to the moon."

He pulls her backwards into his chest,
releases and then applies a headlock.

She feels his bicep tightening around her neck.
At that moment, Ruth pictures Ashley's self-defense demo:
just do this and then this.

44

A blade pierces his stomach twice.
His clamp-like grip loosens.
Ruth stands firm and turns around,
stabbing him again and again in the chest.
She watches him fall in slow motion.

"Police! It's the police!" Ruth hears voices from the stairs,
rumblings that sound like a train arriving.
She releases the pocket knife.

The two officers enter the room.
"Police! Don't move!" the first officer says.
Their guns are drawn and pointing at Michael.
The second officer examines the walls.
He turns the lights on.

"Officers, help! She assaulted me," Michael says.

The second officer lowers his weapon,
putting it into a black holster.

He hides his tears with his hand.

"No," Ruth argues.
"Help me," Michael says.
His blood forms a small puddle.
He's lying on the floor, bleeding out.

Tears fall from Ruth's eyes.
She gradually lowers herself to sit on the floor,
her right eye half open, face reddened and bruised.

"Don't you move, Ruth," the first officer orders.

Michael's head rests on the floor.
He stops moving.
Ruth looks at him and seems to smile.

The first officer surveys the bedroom.
"Look at this, sir, an open bloody blade on the floor," he says.
"Bet we find only one set of prints on it."

Ruth sits with her hands balancing her body upwards.
One hand creates bloody fingerprints on the floor.

The second officer extends his hand to her.
"Are you okay?" he asks.

"It's over," Ruth says.

45

"Cuff her," the second officer instructs.

The first officer holsters his gun
and takes out the handcuffs.

Ruth leans forward with her fists raised.

The first officer heads over to Michael,
checking his pulse. He shakes his head.
"No pulse, should we call it in?" the officer inquires.

"Not yet," the second officer says.
"What happened here?"

The first officer marches over to Ruth,
pulls her up, and handcuffs her.
She feels the cold cuffs tighten.

"You have the right to remain silent..." the officer recites.

"Are you hurt?" the second officer interrupts.

"It's a monster," Ruth says. "It's asleep."

"I wish I was here sooner," he says.
Then he retracts his hand,
taking out a silver notebook.

"How did... you know?" she asks.

"We received a 911 call plus
pictures that confirmed the threat," the first officer informs her.

"Pictures?!" Ruth says. "What pictures?"

"Anything you say..." recites the first officer.

"Take a look outside the window," the second officer interrupts.

Ruth takes a few steps, looks outside, and sees
a figure holding a cell phone, happily waving.
Ashley.

The second officer takes his mic and
calls dispatch, "Can I get the coroner?"

The first officer leads Ruth outside the bedroom.
"Anything you say can and will be used..." he reiterates.